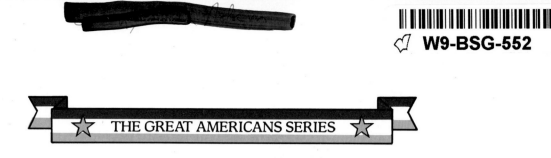

THE GREAT AMERICANS SERIES

Abraham Lincoln

By Kathie Billingslea Smith

Illustrated by James Seward

A Wanderer Book

Published by Simon & Schuster, Inc., New York

Cover Portrait: Sam Patrick

Copyright © 1987 by Ottenheimer Publishers, Inc. All rights reserved including the right of reproduction in whole or in part in any form. Published by WANDERER BOOKS, A Division of Simon & Schuster, Inc. Simon & Schuster Building, 1230 Avenue of the Americas, New York, New York 10020. WANDERER and colophon are registered trademarks of Simon & Schuster, Inc. Printed in Korea.

Also available in Messner Library Edition. ISBN 0-671-64148-4

10 9 8 7 6 5 4 3 2   ISBN: 0-671-62982-4

Abraham Lincoln was born on a cold Sunday morning, February 12, 1809, in western Kentucky. His parents, Thomas and Nancy Hanks Lincoln, were poor, hardworking people. Like other pioneer families, they lived in a one-room log cabin and farmed for a living.

Abraham was named after his grandfather. Little Abraham, or Abe as he was called, was a happy, calm child. He grew very quickly.

"I can hardly sew fast enough to keep him in shirts!" his mother said.

Abe and his elder sister Sally worked hard each day helping on the farm. Whenever they could be spared, they went to school in a one-room log cabin two miles away. Here they sat on benches with children of all ages and learned how to read, spell a few words, and do simple arithmetic. This type of school was called a "blab" school. All of the children recited their lessons aloud at the same time, creating quite a noise! Abe learned quickly and could read and write by the time he was six years old.

School was not free. Abe's parents paid with firewood, or venison, or a bushel of potatoes—any-thing the teacher was willing to accept.

When Abe was seven, his family moved across the Ohio River to the territory of Indiana, which was soon to become a new state. They settled near Little Pigeon Creek and built a crude log cabin eighteen feet square. Abe and Sally slept in a loft just below the roof.

They all lived here happily for two years. Then in 1818, Abe's mother, Nancy, got sick and died. Abe and Sally were very sad and struggled to help do the work that their mother had always done before.

A year later, Thomas Lincoln married a widow who had three children. Her name was Sarah Bush Lincoln, and she loved Abe and Sally very much.

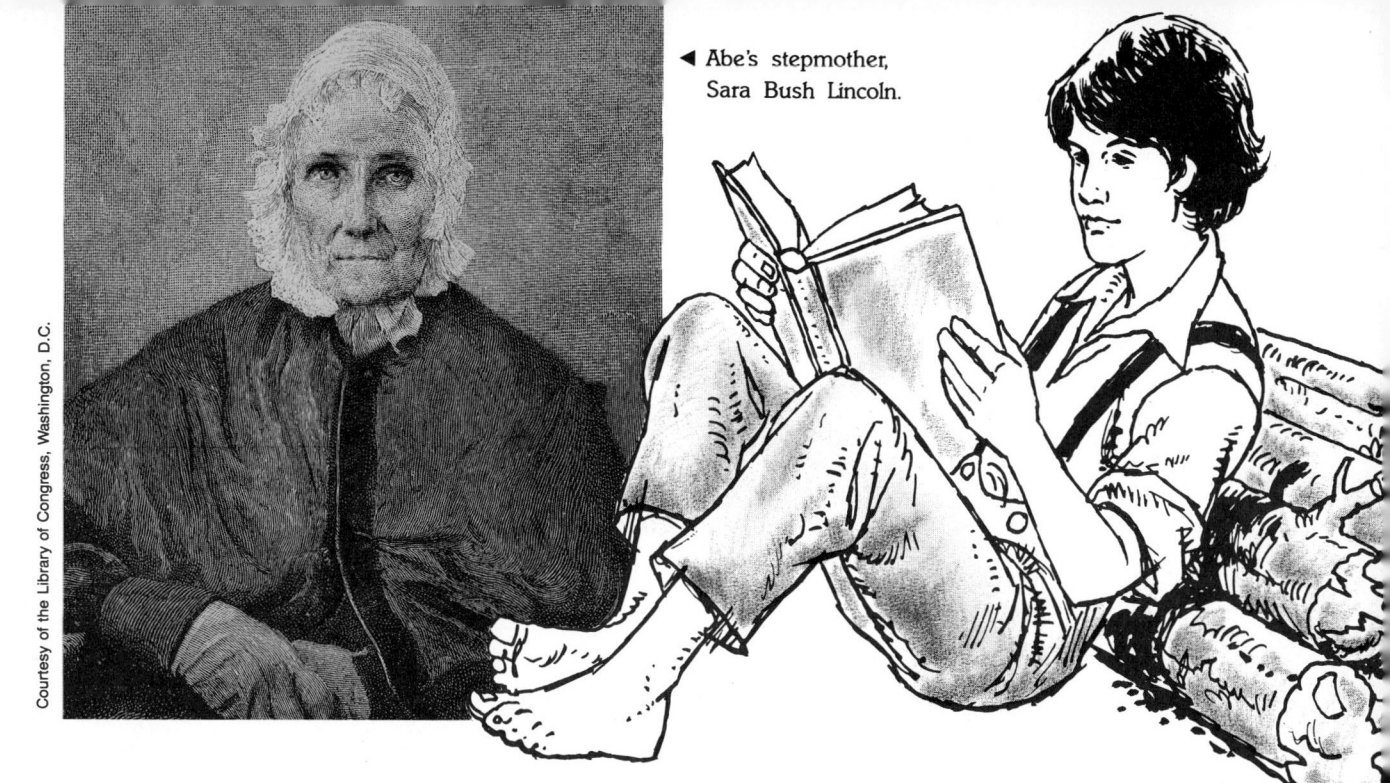

◄ Abe's stepmother,
Sara Bush Lincoln.

She noticed Abe's love of learning and made sure that he went to school at Pigeon Creek as often as he could. At night she let him read by the fireplace long after the others had gone to sleep.

There were no libraries in Indiana then, and very few people owned books. Abe often walked for miles to borrow one to read. "The things I want to know are in books," he claimed. "My best friend is the man who'll give me a book I haven't read."

Once a neighbor lent him a biography of George Washington. Abe eagerly began reading it, then tucked it between two logs in the loft when he went to sleep. That night it rained hard, and the book became water stained. Abe harvested corn for three days to repay his neighbor for the book.

Abe liked people as much as he liked books. He loved to visit in nearby Gentryville and share in the jokes and stories that were such a rich tradition on the frontier. Abe listened and learned well. He remembered and used many of these jokes and tales throughout his life.

By age seventeen, Abe was a tall, strong young man, six feet four inches in height. He became very interested in public speaking and could often be found talking to a crowd of local people. Abe was able to explain complicated ideas in ways everyone could understand.

At age nineteen, Abe was hired to take a flatboat carrying corn, flour, and meat down the Ohio and Mississippi Rivers to the port of New Orleans. This was the first time that Abe had been away from home and on his own. During the three months that he was gone, he never tired of the new sights and sounds that greeted him every day.

But in New Orleans, he was shocked to see black slaves chained together to be sold at auctions. It upset Abe terribly to see people being treated no better than animals.

Slavery was common in the southern states of America. Large plantation owners used slaves to plant and harvest the big crops of tobacco and cotton that were so important to the southern economy. In the northern states, where most people were employed in factories, or shipping and trade, slavery was not so common. Most northern states had voted to abolish slavery. Some northerners, known as Abolitionists, wanted to end slavery in the entire country. But this change could only be made with an amendment to the Constitution of the United States. With northern states voting one way and southern states voting another, no change could be agreed upon.

In 1830, Abe and his family moved to Illinois. Abe and a friend set up a small shop in New Salem. At night when the shop had closed, Abe worked with the village schoolmaster to improve his writing and speaking skills.

But Abe's business failed, leaving him and his partner deeply in debt. Abe worked hard husking corn, splitting logs into fence rails, repairing houses, and writing letters and deeds to earn money to repay his debt. All over the county, he became known as "Honest Abe."

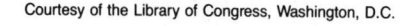

Courtesy of the Library of Congress, Washington, D.C.

In 1834, Abe was elected to represent his county as an Illinois state assemblyman. He spent eight years working in the legislature and studied law on the side. During this time, he became a lawyer and worked in an office in Springfield, Illinois. He was respected by everyone for his fairness and his good nature.

Abe made many close friends. Often at night they would gather around a fireplace and discuss politics. Abe frequently argued with another local attorney and legislator—Stephen A. Douglas. A short man with a large head, Douglas became known as "The Little Giant" because he spoke with such a booming voice.

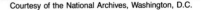
Courtesy of the National Archives, Washington, D.C.

At this time, there were two main political parties, or groups, in the United States: the Whigs and the Democrats. Abe was a member of the Whig Party. They believed that the country needed a strong central government with the power to control business and trade among the states. The Democratic Party, of which Douglas was a member, believed in the right of each state to make its own decisions without interference from the federal government.

Both Abraham Lincoln and Stephen Douglas became well-known for their ability to speak clearly and well in public.

Soon Abe fell in love with Mary Todd, the daughter of a wealthy Kentucky banker. They were married on November 4, 1842, and settled in Springfield. Within a few years, they had two sons, Robert Todd Lincoln and Edward Baker Lincoln.

Abe was kept very busy with his legal work and his government responsibilities. As he walked from place to place, he did not use a briefcase. Instead he carried his bills and important papers in his tall stove-pipe hat!

▲ Abe with his son, Tad

In 1846, Abe was elected to be a representative to the United States Congress. He served for two years and then returned to his law practice in Springfield. In 1850, the Lincolns' four-year-old son, Edward, died. Abe and Mary were grief-stricken and mourned for months. Not long after that, two more sons— William, nicknamed Willie, and Thomas, nicknamed Tad—were born. Their household became a happy, busy place once again.

▲ A slave auction in the South.

Abe became a member of the newly formed Republican Party in 1856. He spoke out more and more against slavery and felt strongly that slavery should not be permitted in new states admitted to the union.

In 1858, he ran against Stephen A. Douglas for the office of United States Senator from Illinois. "The Little Giant" and "Long Abe" were a funny-looking pair of politicians. They held many lively debates. Douglas won the election by a small number of votes. But Abe was known across the country as a leading spokesman for the Republican Party.

In 1860 at the age of fifty-one, Abe was chosen to be the Republican Party's candidate for the Presidency of the United States. His opponent, once again, was Democrat Stephen A. Douglas. This time Abe won, largely with votes from people in the northern states.

People in the southern states were very unhappy to have a president who opposed slavery. Abe knew this and felt that his most important goal was to keep the United States together. He told the southern states that even though he was opposed to slavery, he would let it continue in the south in order to keep the states united.

▲ President Abraham Lincoln being sworn into office in front of the Capitol in Washington, D.C.

Abe spent the next few months preparing to leave Illinois. He sold his horse and buggy and closed up his house. Abe and his family bid goodbye to his elderly stepmother and rode by train to Washington, D.C.

But before Abe was even sworn into office, seven southern states left, or seceded, from the United States and formed a new government called the Confederate States of America. They chose their own president, Jefferson Davis, a former senator from Mississippi. Then the southern states began

to form an army and demanded that the United States soldiers leave the forts in the south.

When the backwoods boy from Kentucky became the sixteenth President of the United States on March 4, 1861, he faced a country split with anger. In his inaugural speech, Lincoln promised to do all he could to "preserve, protect and defend" the United States.

But a month later, in Charleston, South Carolina, the southern troops attacked the United States soldiers that were stationed at Fort Sumter. The Civil War began, with the northern states fighting against the southern states. In some cases, families were split apart as members joined different sides of the fight.

Courtesy of the National Archives, Washington, D.C.

The North had more soldiers, more ships, and more supplies from factories and mines. But the South had a better trained army led by the very skilled General Robert E. Lee. The southern troops also were more familiar with the land where most of the battles were fought.

The war was to rage for four years, and hundreds of thousands of men would be killed. Lincoln was deeply saddened by all of this fighting.

In February, 1862, the Lincolns' eleven-year-old son, Willie, became very sick and died. This was a dark time for the Lincoln family. Abe grieved for his son as well as for the thousands of young men who were dying in the war.

▼ President Lincoln and General McClellan on the battlefield at Antietam in 1862.

On January 1, 1863, Lincoln signed the Emancipation Proclamation. This important law freed all of the slaves in the Confederate states. The slaves rejoiced in their freedom, and many black soldiers later joined the Northern army to fight against the South.

One of the war's bloodiest battles was fought in July, 1863, at Gettysburg, Pennsylvania. The North won, but in three days of fighting, 23,000 of its men were killed or wounded. The Confederate army lost 28,000 men. Soldiers wearing the gray uniforms of the south and the blue uniforms of the north were buried together in the battlefield.

A few months later, that battle site was declared a National Cemetery. The grounds were dedicated in memory of the fallen soldiers. It was here that Lincoln gave his most famous speech, now known as the Gettysburg Address. Lincoln pledged that the United States would "have a new birth of freedom" and that the "government of the people, by the people, for the people, shall not perish from the earth."

Lincoln was re-elected President of the United States in 1864. The war continued as General Ulysses S. Grant led the army of the north deeper into the south.

National Portrait Gallery, Smithsonian Institution, Washington, D.C.

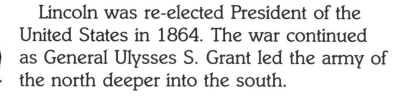

▲ Ulysses S. Grant outside his tent.

On April 8, 1865, after four years of fighting, General Lee surrendered to General Grant in the courthouse at Appomattox, Virginia. The Civil War was finally over! The southern states agreed to stop fighting and rejoin the United States of America.

But the problems of wartime were not over. The South needed to be rebuilt. Many of its cities had been burned. Its economy was ruined. Thousands of its young men had died, and many freed blacks had no homes or jobs.

▲ Robert E. Lee

At the war's end, some people in the North felt
that the South should be punished. But Lincoln in-
sisted on working for "a just and lasting peace"
among the states. At his first public ap-
pearance after the war's end, Lincoln
spoke briefly to the crowd that had
gathered at the White House. Then he

asked the band to play "Dixie," the favorite song of the Southerners.

"I have always thought 'Dixie' one of the best tunes I have ever heard," he said.

On Good Friday, April 14, 1865, after a long day of work, Abe and Mary Lincoln and two friends went to see a play at Ford's Theatre in Washington, D.C. They sat in the President's box near the stage. Midway through the play, Lincoln's bodyguard left for a few minutes to visit with a friend. While the box was unguarded, a man named John Wilkes Booth slipped in and shot Lincoln in the back of the head. Then he leaped onto the stage and ran out of the theater.

Lincoln was carried to a nearby house where he died at seven o'clock the next morning. Less than a week had passed since the end of the Civil War.

Lincoln's funeral was held at the White House. Then his body lay in state in the Capitol building. Thousands of people came for one last look at this great man. Finally his body was put on a train and taken back to Springfield, Illinois to be buried.

Lincoln's Vice-President, Andrew Johnson, became the new President of the United States. He worked to rebuild the South and unite the states once again. But without Abraham Lincoln's strong, sensitive leadership, the struggle was a long, difficult one.

Today, Abraham Lincoln is remembered as a wise, caring leader who guided his country through its worst crisis and helped it truly become the United States of America.